To Dodo

First published 1988 by Walker Books Ltd
87 Vauxhall Walk, London SE11 5HJ

This edition published 2002

2 4 6 8 10 9 7 5 3 1

Text © 1988 A.N. Wilson
Illustrations © 1988 Sarah Fox-Davies

The right of A.N. Wilson and Sarah Fox-Davies
to be identified as author and illustrator respectively
of this work has been asserted by them in accordance
with the Copyright, Designs and Patents Act 1988

This book has been typeset in Garamond

Printed in Hong Kong

British Library Cataloguing in Publication Data:
a catalogue record for this book is available from the British Library

ISBN 0-7445-9411-1

THE *Tabitha* STORIES

A. N. WILSON

illustrated by SARAH FOX-DAVIES

WALKER BOOKS
AND SUBSIDIARIES
LONDON • BOSTON • SYDNEY

In The Beginning...

Old Pufftail was a street cat. He was very proud and very alone. Some cats live with people in their houses. The people give them milk and food in little dishes. They light fires to keep the cats warm in winter. In summer they put out chairs in their gardens for the cats to sit on. The people call this "owning" cats.

But Old Pufftail accepts no two-footer as his owner. He wanders up and down the street getting food where he can find it. When he finds the food in dustbins, the people shout *"Dis-gusting!"* And when he finds the food in people's houses, they call this "stealing". Pufftail just calls it finding food.

Old Pufftail has known many beautiful female cats and he is the father of many cats. But his favourite cat in all the world was a small grey tabby cat, ribbed with mackerel stripes all over her back and face, and with a chest as white and as thick as snow. This beautiful cat was called Tammy. One terrible day, just after  she had given birth to four of Pufftail's kittens, Tammy was run over by a car. Pufftail hates cars and calls them "engines of murder".

Pufftail knew that life, if you are a cat, is a sad business. Even so, he was not prepared for the bad news which Rocket gave him a few days after Tammy's death.

Rocket was a fat, insolent ginger tom cat who often had fights with Pufftail but never came out of them with much dignity.

Old Pufftail was a street cat.

Nevertheless, Rocket considered himself Pufftail's superior. Not only did he live in a comfortable house with a very kind owner, he also had a very happy arrangement with the people at Number Thirteen. Rocket called Number Thirteen his "club", and he often waddled off there for a second dinner if he felt inclined. Rocket's chief pleasure, however, was not eating, but gossip. He loved to pass on news, but it was always bad news, and usually turned out to be untrue.

"Good morning, Pufftail," said Rocket, looking as if he had some very interesting news indeed.

At first Pufftail did not see Rocket. He just heard his annoying voice somewhere overhead. Then, looking up, he saw the ginger tom in the branches of the apple tree in the garden of Number Seventeen.

"So your brats have finally been disposed of," said Rocket, grinning.

"Brats?" asked Pufftail with a show of indifference which he did not feel. "I did not know that I had any brats."

"The kittens at Number Eighteen," said Rocket. "Drowned. Never trust a two-footer, that's what I say."

"No," Pufftail corrected him. "That's what *I* say. You got it from me."

"Common knowledge," grinned Rocket. "I'm just off to the club for a bite to eat. I wish you could join me, but they like a cat to be *clean* at the club. You should look after yourself, old chap. You are starting to look underfed – the Siamese opposite said she thought you looked *scraggy*!"

"I breakfasted extremely well," said Pufftail, trying to keep his temper.

"My bet is they've already drowned those little kits, poor brats," said Rocket.

Pufftail could endure no more. He snarled. He hissed. And then he threw himself at Rocket. But Rocket was quite quick on his toes. Before Pufftail could grab him, he had jumped over a wall and was disappearing into the safety of Number Thirteen, with a "You're a bit edgy, old boy. Hungry, I expect."

Later that day, Pufftail discovered that none of the kind but foolish people who lived in the street had drowned his kittens. Three of the kittens remained at Number Eighteen, where they were born. And the fourth had gone next door, to Number Sixteen. The two-footers at Number Sixteen had not drowned this fourth kitten. Pufftail heard them cooing and drooling over her, as people do when they are cat lovers.

"Do you think he knows that Tabitha is his kitten?"

The fourth kitten looked very like her mother Tammy. She had the same grey mackerel stripes all over her back and tail, and the same thick white chest. The people in the house called her Tabitha. Old Pufftail watched through the window. Day by day and week by week he kept an eye on the little kitten as she grew bigger and stronger.

Pufftail was still very angry that Rocket had alarmed him so much with the story of someone drowning his kittens.

One day, when the people at Number Sixteen were indoors playing with Tabitha, and Pufftail was on a window-ledge outside, looking in at them, he heard someone say, "There's Old Pufftail, looking through the window."

"Do you think he knows that Tabitha is his kitten?" asked a girl.

"Of course," said one two-footer.

But another said, "I shouldn't think he cares. There he goes, waving his thick tail. He never stays in the same place for long."

"Where is he going?" asked the girl.

"Oh," said the older voice, "he's going hunting, by the look of him."

This was nearly true. Pufftail was going to sit by the back door of the "club" until Rocket staggered out, full of his second dinner.

"Our *house now, is it?*" laughed Rocket.

Tabitha And The Other Kitten

When Tabitha had been living in her new home for a few weeks, she noticed that she was not the only cat in the house. There was another kitten which peered in at some of the smaller windows and made faces at her. It even tried to scratch her with its little white paws.

Tabitha was afraid of this kitten.

She wished it was not there. It spoiled her fun to know that whenever she looked out of one of the small windows, this Other Kitten would be there, peering at her with a frightening expression.

It was only when she was indoors that this other cat stared at her. In the garden, it was different. There were plenty of other cats in the garden, but this particular, annoying little cat was never seen there by Tabitha.

Tabitha began to ask the other cats in the garden whether they had seen this annoying new kitten.

She asked Rocket, who lived nearby, and often came to sit on the garden wall. "Rocket," she said, "have you seen a little tabby and white cat coming in and out of our house?"

"*Our* house now, is it?" laughed Rocket.

"Yes," said Tabitha. "But have you? Have you seen her?"

"What sort of cat?" asked Rocket. "Is it a Siamese? There are too many cats in this street altogether. Did you know that there was a Siamese at Number Forty-One who has cat flu? If that spreads down the road, we shall all be done for."

Tabitha had heard neither of cat flu nor of Number Forty-One.

"I don't think it is Siamese," she said. "It is grey – well, tabby and white – with a silly little tail."

"Rather like you, perhaps," said Rocket rudely.

"I don't really know," said Tabitha. "I don't know what I look like."

"It sounds an ordinary little thing," said Rocket. "Too ordinary to notice." And then, rather suddenly, Rocket jumped down from the wall and disappeared. The reason for his sudden departure was the arrival of Pufftail. Tabitha knew that Rocket and Pufftail were not the closest of friends.

"I was asking Rocket," said Tabitha, "about this Other Kitten who keeps bothering me through windows."

And she told her father everything.

"Is it a girl cat or a boy cat?" asked her father with sudden interest.

"It's an *It* cat," said Tabitha. "It spoils things. I was so happy when I was in the house all by myself."

"Then you should frighten it away," said Pufftail. "I am very good at frightening other cats, and I will give you a lesson.

First you must learn to hiss.

Like thisssss."

Tabitha tried to
hiss
like her father.

"And you must arch your back,"
said Pufftail.
"And
you must
hold
your
tail
upright
as if it were
a poker,
and you must allow yourself
to turn to gooseflesh so that all your fur stands on end.
That's right!
You see,
it makes you look
twice
your size!
When you
fluff yourself out,
you look almost like me!
Then you must tell this cheeky little kit
that it must run along or you will bite its ears."

And Pufftail rubbed his own half-bitten ear with a paw and
frowned thoughtfully. And when he had given Tabitha this advice,
old Father Pufftail walked off down the garden path thinking that

he would look to see what the people in the house had thrown into the dustbins that morning. Before long he was contenting himself with a nutritious, slightly rotten mutton bone.

Tabitha went back into the house, resolved to do what her father had told her. She felt nervous about it. After all, what if the kitten came *through* one of the windows and bit *her* ear before she had a chance to hiss and be frightening?

Once inside the house, Tabitha looked about. There was no sign of the Other Kitten in the kitchen. Tabitha sniffed at the tinned food which some kind person had put out for her on a saucer. But it had gone stale and she avoided it. Then she sniffed at the milk in the other saucer. That had gone cheesy, which was the way Tabitha liked it. She lapped it up. And then she left the kitchen and went to play in the little room at the end of the hall.

There was a well in this room where the people liked to come and sit. When there was no one on the well, Tabitha liked to jump on the well seat and walk around. There was water in the well, but it was too far down to drink. When she got thirsty, Tabitha jumped across from the well to the wash-basin. Sometimes there was water coming out of the taps in gently drinkable droplets. But just as she was thinking how much she would like to drink a drip from the tap Tabitha looked up at the little framed window over the wash-basin. And there *It* was: the Other Kitten, staring at her.

What was it that old Father Pufftail had advised? She must hiss and make her fur stand on end and make her little tail stand up

There was no sign of the Other Kitten in the kitchen.

straight and tall like a poker. All of a sudden, Tabitha felt too scared to do any of these things, and she jumped down from the basin and ran along the hall.

She went to the sitting room and stood on top of the piano. There seemed to be a large window above the piano with a golden frame around it. But Tabitha had no sooner got to the top of the piano, than she saw *It* staring at her again! It looked almost as scared as she felt. Tabitha wondered, if she managed one really frightening hiss, whether she could frighten the kitten away. So Tabitha held her tail in the air and pretended it was a poker. And she made all her fur stand on end. And she was just about to hiss, like *thissssss,* when, oh mercy!

The Other Kitten had had the same idea. When Tabitha raised her tail, It raised Its tail. And when Tabitha fluffed out her fur and tried to look cross, It looked even fluffier and even crosser. And Tabitha was so frightened by the sight of It that she forgot to hiss, like *thissss.* She jumped down from the piano and ran upstairs to one of the bedrooms.

There were a number of windows in the bedroom. Tabitha, very cautiously, looked through one of them. She saw the street with cars parked along it. She saw the tree-tops and she saw the little gardens. Surely she was too high up for the Other Kitten to come peering at her?

But on the other side of the bedroom was another window. This window did not look out into the street, it looked through into

another bedroom, very like Tabitha's bedroom. It had a chest of drawers, and a large brass bed and two lamps.

And horror of horrors! Across this other brass bed, Tabitha could see the Other Kitten stalking along, as if It belonged there!

Tabitha watched It very closely. It stopped and peered at her. Once more It raised Its tail and fluffed out Its fur. And then... It hissed. Like *thisssssss!*

Tabitha was very frightened. But she was also very, very cross.

This was her patch, and *thisssssss* It did not belong there! How dare It come and *hisssssss* at her in her bedroom? Was she not Tabitha, and was not Pufftail her father? Anger inspired her now, and she tossed herself furiously against the glass.

The Other Kitten did the same, clawing against the glass and making very angry faces at Tabitha.

They could not actually touch one another through the glass, but it was almost as exciting as a real fight.

And then Tabitha began to notice something.

Whenever her paw went up to the glass, the Other Kitten put up its paw. And when Tabitha slowed down her furious clawing, It slowed down also. And she began to realize that this Other Kitten, this annoying little tabby and white kitten on the other side of the glass with a silly tail was ... herself!

She was looking at herself! She raised her tail once more and looked at it. As tails went, she decided that she had been wrong about it. In its way, it was rather distinguished, she decided.

She scampered downstairs, just to make sure by looking at the window over the piano. Yes, there it was – quite a pretty little face once one got used to it – looking at her rather sweetly from the top of the piano. Whenever she smiled, the looking-glass kitten smiled a back-to-front smile.

Tabitha ran into the well room, just to make sure. She jumped on to the wash-basin and looked at the little framed window above it. Yes! There she was! She noticed a smudge on her nose and licked a paw before wiping it clean. The back-to-front kitten did the same.

The next time she met Pufftail, father of many cats, he asked her, "Did you manage to frighten away that cat you were telling me about? The silly-looking one with not much of a tail?"

Tabitha could not tell lies to her father.

"It does not look *that* silly," she said. "But I did as you told me. I hissed. And I fluffed out my fur, and I held up my tail as straight as a poker. And I do not think that I shall ever be troubled by that really rather pretty little cat ever again."

So that was that. But for weeks afterwards, Rocket was telling the other cats in the road that there were two kittens at Number Sixteen and that there was very bad blood between them.

She was looking at herself!

They kindly provided Tabitha with a nice large brass bed.

TABITHA AND THE CAGE

The people who looked after Tabitha had always been kind to her, ever since she was a tiny kitten.

"Two-footers are not always kind," warned Pufftail her father. "You will see."

But, as Tabitha grew up, she did not see. The people seemed so very kind, and so very foolish! And then everything changed, and she began to wonder whether Pufftail was not right after all.

Of course, in the happy, early days of her kittenhood, Tabitha learnt that people could be very clumsy and very annoying. For instance, they kindly provided Tabitha with a nice large brass bed in which she could snooze: much nicer than the thing they filled up with cushions and placed on the kitchen floor, and called the "cat basket". But sometimes, just when Tabitha was getting comfortable on her large brass bed, the kind but foolish people tried to get into the bed too. She knew that they were only trying to provide her with some warmth: they were being human hot water-bottles, and it was very kind of them. But she found it annoying!

Then again, the people sometimes played foolish games. If she decided not to sleep on her bed, she would sometimes sit in the dear little nest which they put out for her on one of their tables. It was a metal nest just Tabitha's size, and it was a perfect place to sleep. When Tabitha woke up, there were amusing twiddly bits which she could play with and, sometimes, even a piece of paper in the nest which Tabitha could chew. But then, just when she was enjoying herself, Tabitha would hear someone call out, "Oh, TABITHA! You are sleeping in my typewriter!" And the woman would then start to hit the nest with her fingers which made the metal twiddly bits wriggle about. Most uncomfortable for Tabitha.

Tabitha would then like to jump out of the nest and look for somewhere else to sleep. The crinkly blanket was a good place. But if the man found Tabitha on the crinkly blanket, he would call out, "Oh TABITHA! Get off my newspaper!"

Tabitha knew that he was only trying to be amusing. And when she was amused, Tabitha would chew the crinkly blanket, or scrumple it with her sharp claws. It made a lovely noise.

But everything was changing now and Tabitha thought of her wise old father's words: "Two-footers are not always kind."

One day, the woman and her two children came into the kitchen carrying a large bag of hay.

"This will make an admirable bed for her," said the woman.

A bed? Was the new idea that Tabitha should sleep on a bed of hay like an animal in a farmyard?

"What about her food?" asked one of the children.

"Yes," thought Tabitha, "what about my food?"

Up to this point, the people had been quite kind about feeding Tabitha. There was a big white box in the corner of the kitchen. Even on the hottest summer day, inside that box it was winter. The people kept delicious things in the box – butter to lick, raw

lamb chops (how they had squealed with excitement when Tabitha showed them how to eat a raw lamb chop) and delicious creamy milk which they sometimes poured into a saucer for Tabitha and sometimes – to make it more amusing – put into a jug on a dresser so that, before she drank it, Tabitha could walk along the shelf and make a jingly-jangly music as she swished her tail from side to side.

One day, when Tabitha was quite a young kitten, she had taught the people a good game which can be played with a roast chicken. Someone puts a roast chicken on the table. Then Tabitha pretends that the chicken is alive. She plays "hunt the bird" and pounces on it. How they squealed when she taught them this game. They sounded most appreciative. And, like any cat, Tabitha eats some vegetables. That is, if she is strolling on the grass in the garden, she will nibble a few blades. On colder days, when she is not feeling like a walk in the garden, she eats the flowers which are kindly put out for her in a jug on the sitting room table. She had never much enjoyed these flowers, but she had always tried not to hurt the people's feelings.

But now they were going to hurt *her* feelings very much indeed.

"What *will* she eat?" asked the child who was carrying the hay.

"I think she would like some raw cabbage," said the woman.

Raw cabbage? Had the people gone mad? Hay to sleep on! Cabbage to eat! Who did they think she was?

Tabitha went out into the garden. Her tail was very high. She felt too angry and too puzzled to think of anything but the hay and the cabbage. She did not even bother to chase a little sparrow who was hopping, quite close to her, on the lawn.

"I will not eat cabbage," she said, to no one in particular. "Nor will I sleep on hay."

Rocket, the marmalade cat, stood on the garden wall and looked down on her with an air of condescension.

"Changing your diet, are they?" he asked. "I expect they have run out of money. I knew it would ruin them, feeding you on chops and chicken."

Tabitha maintained a dignified silence.

"Did you see them bringing in that hay?" Rocket went on. "I heard them say it would make a nice bed."

Tabitha still said nothing.

Then Rocket grinned wider and said, "All I can say is, I'm very glad that my servant does not intend to keep me locked in a cage. That's what they are going to do to you, you know. I heard them talking about it."

And he jumped down on his side of the wall and disappeared.

Locked in a cage? This was terrible!

Rocket had a nasty habit of telling bad news with a grin on his face. Sometimes he got things wrong. But today, Tabitha was not so sure. She slunk down to the bottom of the garden to consider what to do next. There was a little shed there, pleasantly shady on hot afternoons and out of the wind and rain in bad weather. Tabitha often went there for contemplation.

There were two ways to the shed: the boring way, trodden by people, and the interesting way, trodden by cats.

The boring way was along the path and through the arbour on to the little terrace. The interesting way was up the trellis and along the roof of the shed. This was the way trodden by Tabitha. As she went, she was thinking, very hard. If the people were planning to lock her up in a cage, then she must escape.

But surely Rocket was wrong. Or was he?

As she jumped down from the roof of the shed, she saw what Rocket had been talking about. She could see the cage, put quite openly in the garden.

Tabitha walked up to the cage and looked at it more closely.

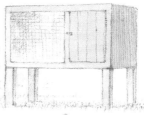

Even when she was a tiny kitten, she would have found the cage much too small and cramped for her requirements. Now... for a grown cat to be put into such a thing... it was impossible! She would not fit!

Tabitha was indignant.

First they bought hay and expected her to use it as a bed. Then they chopped up cabbage stalks and expected her to eat them. Now they intended to put her in a cage. It was the final indignity. There was nothing for it. Tabitha decided that she must run away.

First, however, she thought that she would go back into the house and say goodbye to her favourite spots. She paced round the house looking at all the places where she liked to sleep and play and sit. For the last time, she perched on the back of the sofa and looked out of the window into the street.

She saw her proud old father, Pufftail.

She decided that she would join him and live, as he did, on what he could hunt or steal. Sparrows and thrushes were plentiful in the neighbourhood, and there was an abundance of dustbins.

Tabitha knew that she would prefer to be free like her father – even if it meant being poor and uncomfortable – than to be locked in a cage and fed on raw cabbage.

One last look at the old house and then she would be off to join Pufftail. She scampered round the house. She said goodbye to her large comfortable bed. Now the people would have to sleep there without her.

She said goodbye to the pile of crinkly sheets which the man called his newspapers. She ran downstairs and said goodbye to the metal nest with the twiddly bits with which the woman tried to entertain Tabitha. In those days, the people had been Tabitha's friends. But "two-footers are not always kind."

"Tabitha is running around like a cat on hot bricks," one of the people said.

And another, one of the children, said, "Perhaps she is cross with us for buying a guinea-pig. Tabitha! Tabitha, darling! Where are you?"

The girl found Tabitha and picked her up and took her down to the kitchen. Tabitha knew what this meant. She knew that the girl was about to put her in that cage! She wriggled and she squealed.

"Don't hold her so tightly," said the other child. "She doesn't like it when you pick her up."

"Shut up," said the first child. "I'm just going to show her to Doris. So that they can be friends."

"I hope they won't be *too* friendly," said the woman.

Tabitha blinked a little and surveyed the kitchen scene. Whatever would these people think of next? They had bought a firm, juicy-looking creature with bright eyes and glossy white fur. They called this pig Doris.

The people drooled over Doris – somewhat foolishly, Tabitha thought. But what was this? They were carrying handfuls of hay out into the garden and putting it into the cage. And one of the girls carried a plastic dish full of those cabbage stalks. And the woman, following behind, carried Doris the guinea-pig and put *her* in the cage! The cage was not meant for Tabitha after all!

When Tabitha came back into the kitchen, the man said to her, "Now, Tabitha, you are to be very good and you must not chase the guinea-pig."

Tabitha smiled at him. People could be very amusing at times. She felt happy. To tell the truth, she was rather glad that she would not, after all, be living a roving, cold life with her father. She saw the advantages of living in a house, with a full family of human servants to look after her.

The man put down a dish of extremely smelly pilchards for Tabitha's tea, and a saucer of milk. After the meal, which was

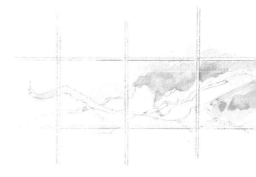

delicious, she asked to be let out, and she strolled into the garden. She walked as cautiously as she could manage. But it was hard not to have a spring in her step as she approached the cage. It was hard not to look at the hutch and the bright, beady little eyes which were staring out of the round, plump little body of the guinea-pig.

Tabitha was glad that the pig, and not she, was in the cage. She was also glad that she had just eaten all those pilchards, which took the edge off her appetite. That plump, juicy little body did look very appetizing indeed. But, perhaps, instead of being something to eat, Doris would become a friend.

Betty was a fluffy white creature.

A Visit From Betty

Tabitha was glad that Doris had come. Before Doris came, Tabitha had been rather lonely. She did not realize at the time that she had been lonely; but she had often jumped up on to the garden wall, and wandered up and down upon it, just hoping to see someone, anyone, for a bit of a chat. She had even half looked forward to disagreeable encounters with Betty, the proud little white cat, who had come to replace Tabitha's mother at Number Eighteen. Betty was a fluffy white creature, who looked more like a thing to powder your nose with than an animal. But underneath her pretty exterior, she was savage and fierce. Tabitha did not always enjoy meeting Betty, and now she did not have to worry whether she met Betty or not; because there was Doris.

The summer had come. The sun shone brightly, and the grass on the lawn grew thick and green. The children made a "run" on the lawn, out of chicken wire, where Doris could run up and down in the fresh air. It was nicer than her stuffy little hutch. The sides of the run were much too high for the guinea-pig to climb. But they were not too high for a cat to jump!

Sometimes the children went out, leaving Doris in the run and Tabitha to stand guard. Tabitha was pleased to be left alone with her new friend. If you are an animal, you do not always want people about, and she looked forward to getting to know Doris really well.

Tabitha began by describing her birth at Number Eighteen.

"My father," she added with justifiable pride, "is Pufftail, who sometimes walks up and down the garden path. You will have seen him, I expect. But you, Doris, what about you? You came from a pet shop, I believe?"

Tabitha certainly did not mean to offend Doris by saying that she came from a shop. But Doris said nothing in reply. She simply puffed out her cheeks and stared at Tabitha with her bright beady eyes.

"Oh, dear," thought Tabitha. "I hope I have not offended my friend Doris."

Doris had a mouthful of grass. She chewed and chewed, quite rapidly. Then, still staring with her bright beady eyes, she said, "You was saying?"

"I was saying," said Tabitha, "that I heard you had come from a shop? A pet shop?"

"Oh?" said Doris.

Cats are deliberately mysterious. Guinea-pigs are not. Doris was not trying to keep her earlier life a secret from Tabitha. She had forgotten all about it. She had forgotten the pet shop. She had forgotten being chosen from the window by the children. She had forgotten being put into her hutch. Doris, in fact, forgot anything which happened to her more than five minutes before.

She looked with greed at a cabbage stalk, which the children had thrown into the run, and then she started to munch it.

"I eats my salad," she said, with a full mouth, "and I looks about."

"I'm very glad you *do* look about," said Tabitha. "Cats do not eat salad..."

"Oh, ar?" said Doris, not very interested, and still chewing.

"In fact," said Tabitha, "apart from a little grass now and again..."

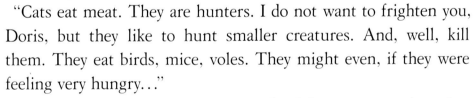

"I likes grass," said Doris.

"Cats eat meat. They are hunters. I do not want to frighten you, Doris, but they like to hunt smaller creatures. And, well, kill them. They eat birds, mice, voles. They might even, if they were feeling very hungry..."

Tabitha looked at Doris with pity. She did not want to alarm her friend, but she did want to *warn* her.

"No," said Doris. "I likes a nice bit of salad." She chomped rapidly. "I eats my salad, like I say, and I looks about."

"Do look about please,"
said Tabitha, and
she left Doris for a while
enjoying her cabbage.

Tabitha went down
to the little arbour
at the end of the garden
and climbed the trellis.
Then she walked along
the wall and tried to catch
a few butterflies who were
fluttering in the buddleia.

Then she jumped down over the wall and met Rocket.

"Looking for Betty?" he asked, with a grin.
"I understand you two have struck up a friendship."

"Not really," said Tabitha.

"A beautiful creature," said Rocket. "What a beautiful little
creature she is."

Tabitha supposed that it all depended on what you considered
beautiful. The larger people in her house sometimes said Betty
was beautiful.

"That red collar she wears is truly fetching," said Rocket.

"You mean her flea collar?" said Tabitha.

Just at that moment, from the direction of her garden, Tabitha
heard a terrible squealing and screeching.

"Hello," said Rocket with a smile, "sounds like trouble."

Tabitha jumped up on to the wall and looked down at the lawn. She saw the little run and the cabbage stalks. She saw Doris. She also saw Betty, who was just about to pounce on Doris. Betty had got into the run and had cornered Doris. Poor little Doris was letting out high-pitched squeaks.

Tabitha jumped down. All the fur on her back and tail stood on end, and she looked really fierce. She hissed at Betty and told her to go away.

"This is my snack," hissed Betty. "I found her first. Now don't spoil a girl's sport. Just run along, darling, won't you?"

"Get out of that run," hissed Tabitha.

But Betty would not get out of the run. She advanced on Doris, slowly, ever so slowly, staring at her so persistently that the poor little guinea-pig was hypnotized.

Tabitha jumped over the wire meshing and flung herself at Betty. Betty stuck out her claws and cuffed Tabitha in the face, giving her a nasty cut on the side of her nose. But Tabitha stood

Tabitha stood her ground.

her ground. She, too, stuck out her claws. She cuffed Betty in the face and hissed and spat at her.

"Oh, *really,* darling, if you're going to be *silly,*" said Betty, with a snarl, and she jumped out of the run and scampered off to the bottom of the garden.

Tabitha sighed. She licked her paw and rubbed her sore nose and smiled at Doris, who was gibbering in the corner of the run.

"That was a near escape," said Tabitha. "You really must keep a sharp look-out, and squeak if you hear a cat coming. Another cat, that is," said Tabitha.

"Tabitha! Tabitha!" said an agitated person coming down the path at the side of the house. "Get out of the run this instant!"

Tabitha jumped out of the run and went to sit on top of the garden shed, while the children shouted at her. They told her she was a naughty girl for getting into the run and scaring poor Doris. They did not know Tabitha had driven away Betty and saved Doris's life. Doris had already forgotten the incident and was scurrying up and down the run as fast as her very short legs would carry her plump little body.

Later that afternoon, Tabitha went to say hello to her through the meshing.

"People don't understand much," mused Tabitha. But then, looking at Doris, she thought, "Neither do guinea-pigs."

"I eats my salad," said Doris, in the middle of a contented mouthful, "and I looks about."

Where Is Tabitha?

"Tabitha looks pleased with herself," remarked the woman of the house one day.

"She always does," said her husband.

"She looks like a cat that's got the cream," said the woman.

Tabitha smiled. She wished that she had been drinking some cream. Certainly she was getting plump, as though she had drunk cream by the gallon. Not long before, Tabitha had been a thin, almost a skinny, little cat. She had thin white paws and a skinny little grey body covered with mackerel stripes. Betty, next door, had even been heard to ask Tabitha what *was* that thing at the end of her body–was it a tail or a pipe-cleaner? Tabitha had tried not to hear. She minded being thought too thin. But she was not thin any more.

She had begun to get stouter during the months of summer. By day, when the children were out at school, Tabitha had snoozed in some favourite spot, lying on the bed in a pool of warm sunshine

or perched on top of the piano. When darkness fell, Tabitha liked to prowl out on to the window ledge and trample on the flowers in the window box and call out to her neighbours. Not all her neighbours were as rude as Betty or as unreliable as Rocket. There was the magnificent dark Shenouda from Number Twelve. There were Sheba and Jason from Number Fifteen, a noble pair. And there were her brothers who still lived at Number Eighteen, two fluffy marmalade fellows with whom she liked to play by the light of the summer moon.

But in the summer moonlight, other cats came–strange cats from far away–to visit Tabitha. Better than any of them, she liked a mysterious black stranger with bright eyes, who called to see her night after night. And then he went away, never to be seen again.

That had all been a long time ago, when Tabitha was still a thin little cat and the nights were short and warm. The evenings were chillier now and came shortly after tea. Tabitha went out into the garden much less often. She stayed indoors and ran up and down the house. She went into the larder and rummaged under the shopping basket there.

She went into the cupboard under the stairs and made a very great clatter with buckets and fishing rods and vacuum cleaners.

She poked about the wardrobes in each of the bedrooms as though she were searching for a hat to wear to a party. She did find a pile of hats–and one of them fell on her head; but it did not suit her.

She liked a mysterious black stranger with bright eyes.

She got into the airing cupboard and upset the neat piles of sheets and towels. And then she really did smile like a cat who had got the cream. She smiled and she smiled.

"This," thought she, "will do admirably. It is warm and clean."

And then she paced about the house, smiling more mysteriously than ever.

The days went by, and with each day that passed, Tabitha became a little plumper and her smile became a little more mysterious as she slept by the hissing gas fire. It was autumn now. And then, one day, when the children looked for Tabitha in the kitchen, she was not there.

They put down a saucer of milk, but Tabitha did not come to drink it.

They put down a dish of smelly food – so smelly that they wrinkled up their noses. It was Tabitha's favourite, but she did not come to eat it.

"Where is Tabitha?"

"Tabitha is lost!"

They looked in the garden. "Tabitha! Tabitha!"

They looked in the garden shed, but she was not there. Rocket was standing on the garden wall.

"Have you seen Tabitha?" the children asked.

Rocket grinned at them, as though they were being silly. He had already told old Pufftail that Tabitha had gone missing and was believed to have been stolen by a family of roving gypsies.

But Rocket said nothing to the children.

They met old Pufftail making his stately way down the garden path, like a lion walking through the jungle.

"Pufftail, oh Pufftail, have *you* seen Tabitha?" they asked him. But he was not going to repeat Rocket's foolish story of the gypsies. He hissed at the children and ran out of their way.

The children went back indoors and searched in all Tabitha's favourite places. They looked on top of the piano. They looked on the brass bed. They looked in their mother's typewriter and on their father's newspaper. But they could not find Tabitha.

They looked in their own bedrooms. They looked in the bath.

Tabitha could hear them calling, but she did not move or stir. She smiled to herself, a broader smile than ever and she thought how clever she had been to find this warm cupboard so full of nice towels. That morning, Tabitha had stopped being such a plump little cat. Curled up beside her in the cupboard were four tiny kittens with their eyes tight shut.

One of the kittens was a tabby like herself. One was black and white. And two of the kittens were coal black. Already Tabitha was expecting that when the coal black kittens opened their eyes, they would be bright and shining, like her coal black visitor of the summer.

All five of them were tired and warm and happy, Tabitha and her four kittens. Tabitha was right. The airing cupboard made an admirable nursery.

The airing cupboard made an admirable nursery.

A.N. WILSON is a confirmed cat lover, saying, "I can think
of many ways in which I would be a better person
if I were more like my cats, but I cannot think of a single way
in which my cats would be better for being more like me."
A distinguished novelist, biographer and journalist,
A.N. Wilson has won several prestigious awards. His first book
featuring cats, *Stray*, was about Tabitha's father, Pufftail.
Another of his animal stories, *Hazel the Guinea-pig*,
is also published by Walker.

SARAH FOX-DAVIES is a highly respected illustrator
who is renowned for her paintings of nature and animals.
She has illustrated numerous books for children,
including *Little Caribou* (which she also wrote);
Walk with a Wolf (shortlisted for The Times Educational
Supplement Information Book of the Year Award);
Little Beaver and the Echo (shortlisted for the Children's
Book Award); *Bat Loves the Night*; and *The Snow Bears*.
Sarah lives in Wales.